P9-DDV-306

To: ~~Steve~~ + Mary ~~⬛⬛⬛⬛~~

From: St. Thomas More

Copyright © MCMLXXXIX
by Susan Squellati Florence
Published by the C.R. Gibson Company
Norwalk, Connecticut 06856
Printed in the United States of America
All rights reserved
ISBN 0-8378-1875-3

A GIFT OF TIME

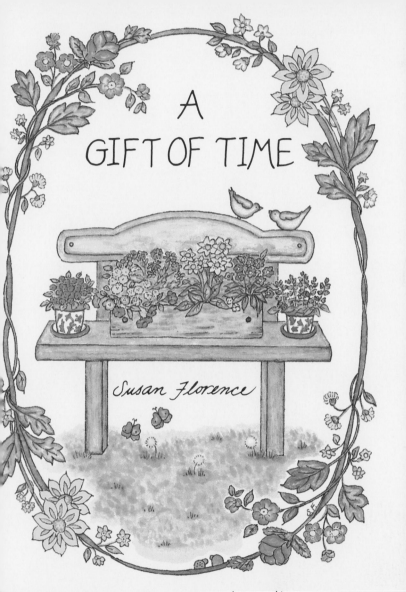

Susan Florence

The C.R. Gibson Company, Norwalk, Ct. 06856

Now is the time to stop
and watch the sun's rays
as they sparkle
through the windows
of our lives.

Now is the time
to listen
to each other.

Now is the time
to talk about
our deepest
           desires,
to hold hands
with each others
           dreams...

to share
the joy
and sadness
held within
our lives.

Now is the time
to put aside
the chatter
of small things...
and to know
that time
is all we have.

Now is the time
to celebrate
the small joys
of this day ...

to notice
the light
and the shadows.

It may be time
to dance ...
It may be time
to grieve ...

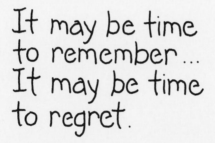

It may be time
to remember...
It may be time
to regret.

It may be time
to forgive
It may be time
to forget.

Yesterday
is always with us
yet yesterday
is always gone .

Tomorrow
rides on the horizon
like a bird on the wing.
Tomorrow
is a flower opening,
a butterfly emerging
from its cocoon.

Today is fullness
like a fruit
when it is ripe,
like a benevolent rose
fully opened
        to the sun,
        to the rain,
giving of itself entirely.

Today can nourish us
and inspire us
like no other time.

Treasure the moments
of the new dawn,
of the dew on the lawn,
of the sun's journey
through the sky.

And after
the crimson light
has fallen...

when only
the lavender hue
of first night remains,
as the stars begin
their ritual twinkle ...

let our hearts
touch
and be full
of thanks ...

this gift of time
is all we have.